More books about Kipper

Kipper
Kipper's Toybox
Kipper's Birthday
Kipper's Snowy Day
Kipper's Christmas Eve
Kipper and Roly
Kipper's Monster
Kipper's Beach Ball
One Year with Kipper
Hide Me, Kipper
Kipper Story Collection
Kipper's Birthday
and Other Stories

We won't
need you
till much,
much later.

First published in 2000
by Hodder Children's Books

This edition published in 2014

Text and illustrations copyright © Mick Inkpen 2000

Hodder Children's Books
338 Euston Road
London NW1 3BH

Hodder Children's Books Australia
Level 17/207 Kent Street
Sydney, NSW 2000

A catalogue record of this book is available
from the British Library.

ISBN: 978 1 444 91814 4
10 9 8 7 6 5 4 3 2 1

Printed in China

Hodder Children's Books is a division of
Hachette Children's Books.
An Hachette UK Company.
www.hachette.co.uk

Mick Inkpen
Kipper's

A to Z

Hodder
Children's
Books

A division of Hachette Children's Books

This is Kipper's little friend, Arnold.
Arnold has found an ant.

Aa is for ant.

And Arnold.

Bb is for box.

And buzzzzzzzzzzzzzzzzzzzzzzzzzzzzzzzzz

They put the ant
in the box,
and followed
the bumblebee.

It flew away.
'Let's find something
beginning with C,'
said Kipper.
But the caterpillar had
already found them!

Cc is for
Crawly caterpillar.

Dd is for duck.

'Duck!' said Arnold.
The duck was too big
to fit into Arnold's box.
And so was the...

enormous

Ee is for empty.

elephant!

Where is the ant?

Ee
is for
elephant.

The frog would have
fitted in Arnold's box,
but Kipper couldn't
catch it.
It was too **f**ast.

Ff is for **frog.**

Arnold was still
wondering where the ant
had gone, when a little,
green grasshopper jumped
straight into his box.
'Good!' said Kipper.

Gg is for
grasshopper.

Hh is for hill and happy.

They skipped all the way to the top

of Big Hill, and down the other side.

Arnold found another interesting insect. He opened his box and put the interesting insect inside.

I i is for insect.

They went home for
a drink of juice.
Arnold helped himself
to some jam too.

J j is for juice.

And a bit of jam too.

Kipper couldn't think of anything beginning with K. Can you think of anything?

K k is for...

L was easy.
Outside there were
lots of ladybirds.
Lots and lots.
Arnold put one
in his box.

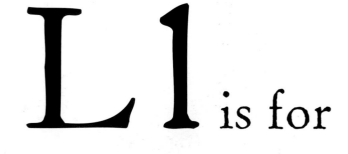

L l is for
lots of ladybirds.

Arnold found some
little muddy mountains.
He was so busy playing
that he didn't even notice
the mole.

M m is for mole

and **mud.**

'Is it my turn now?'
said the zebra.
'No, not now!'
said Kipper.
'You don't
begin with N.'

Nn is for

No, not now!

Arnold climbed on the swing.

Oo is for on...

And then he fell off again.

and **off.** And oo is for oops!

Arnold was upset.
He sat up puffing and
panting and a little pink.
So Kipper took him to
his favourite place.
The pond.

Pp

is for puff, pant, pink

and pond.

Quack!

Quack!

Quack!

Quack!

Is that Arnold's ant?

Quack!

Quack!

Quack!

Qq is for quiet!

And quack of course.

It started to rain.

Rr is for rainbow.

They splashed home
through the puddles.

S s is for

Splish!

Splosh!

Splash!

And six squidgy slugs.

At home Kipper got out his toys.

Tt is for toys.

'I know what begins with U!' said Kipper. 'Umbrella!'
They played under the umbrella, while the rain poured down outside.

Uu is for

Under the umbrella.

'V is very, very hard,'
said Kipper. 'Do you think
we could find a volcano?'
Arnold shook his head.
So they made a picture
of one instead.

Vv is for
volcano!

The rain stopped.
They looked out of the
window to see what
they could see for W.

W w is for

wiggly worm.

But what begins with X?
Kipper thought
and thought
and thought.
He thought of box,
which ends in X, and he
thought of socks,
which doesn't.

'I know!' he said suddenly.
He took out the interesting
insect and said...

X x is for xugglybug!

'It must be my turn
by now!' said the zebra.
'Is it my turn?
Is it?
Is it?'

Yy is for

Yes!

So the zebra stood
in the middle of the page,
and we all said,

Z z is for zebra!

ZZ

ZZZZZZZZ

And for Arnold's little **Z**oo, too.

'My children absolutely LOVE all of Mick Inkpen's books, and I still love reading Kipper to them, even when it's for the hundredth time...'

CRESSIDA COWELL

'He is the perfect pup to grow up with...'

HILARY McKAY

'Storytelling at its best.' DAVID MELLING